A HAPPY ENDING BOOK ™

# Hoppity's first Thunderstorm

by Jane Carruth    illustrated by Tony Hutchings

MODERN PUBLISHING

A Division of Unisystems, Inc.
NEW YORK, NEW YORK 10022
Printed in Belgium

"Watch me, Tufty!" Hoppity cried, as he rode his new scooter around the garden. He had tied Tufty on to the swing so that the little bear could see how clever he was. Just then Mommy called out, "Come in at once, Hoppity. It's nearly time for your bath. And it's starting to rain." But Hoppity pretended not to hear.

Hoppity was having such fun that he hardly noticed the
rain. He didn't even see the big black thunder clouds. Then,
suddenly, the raindrops got bigger and splashier and out
rushed Daddy, looking angry.
"Come inside at once," he shouted. "Your new scooter will
get all rusty if you play with it in the rain!" In the rush to
get indoors, poor little Tufty was forgotten on the swing.

"Wouldn't it be fun if all the raindrops changed into bath bubbles?" Hoppity said, as Mommy got him ready for his bath.

"I don't know what the flowers would say," Mommy laughed. And Hoppity suddenly remembered Tufty. Tufty was still in the garden!

"I must rescue Tufty," he cried. "Please let me get him!" Mommy shook her head. "It's raining far too hard for anyone to go outside," she said firmly.

Hoppity didn't really enjoy his bubble bath because he was thinking about Tufty. And when Mommy tucked him in his bed, he said he wouldn't sleep. "Can Bobtail come and see me?" he asked. "He could read me a story."

"Not now," said Mommy, going to the window to draw the
curtains. "He is busy doing his homework."
"Can you see Tufty out there?" Hoppity asked next. "I
can't sleep without Tufty, you know!"
"It's too dark to see him," said Mommy.

As soon as Mommy kissed Hoppity goodnight and left the
room, Hoppity scrambled out of bed and ran for the door.
He planned to go and get Tufty himself. He couldn't bear to
leave his little friend out there in the garden.

But just as Hoppity was opening the door, there came an enormous, gigantic, crashing bang! He was so scared that he turned back and dived under the bed. There he stayed, shivering with fright, and forgot all about Tufty.

Almost at once Mommy came rushing into the room. Of course she saw Hoppity's little feet sticking out from under the bed. Nevertheless she called out in her best hide-and-seek voice, "Where are you, Hoppity? Where are you hiding? I can't see you!"
At the sound of her voice, Hoppity felt brave.

He came out from under the bed and Mommy gave him a
big hug. "I-I thought it was a giant coming to get me!" he
whispered. "It wasn't, was it?"
"Of course not," said Mommy. "That was thunder! It was
just a loud bang in the sky."

Hoppity still clung to Mommy's dress as she peeked out of
the window. "There will be another clap of thunder soon,"
she said. "I saw lightning just now. It lit up the sky."
"Does lightning hurt?" asked Hoppity.
"Sometimes it can be very dangerous," said Mommy.

"Should you stay indoors when lightning comes?" Hoppity
asked next, as Mommy tidied his bed.
"Yes," said Mommy. "And if you are outside, never shelter
under trees."
Hoppity got out his drum as there came another bang. "I
can bang, too," he laughed, "as loud as thunder!"

Just when Mommy was telling Hoppity that the storm
would soon be over, he remembered Tufty again, and made
a dash for the door. Mommy couldn't stop him but Daddy
did! "What is all the fuss about?" he asked.
"It's Tufty!" Hoppity sobbed. "I must get him!"

"Dear me!" Daddy said. "I do believe you care more about Tufty than your new scooter!"

"Of course he does," said a voice behind Daddy. There was Hoppity's big brother, Bobtail, and he was holding Tufty. "Daddy brought him in before the thunderstorm," he explained.

Hoppity was so happy to see Tufty again that he jumped straight into bed. Mommy was soon there with a hot chocolate and some cookies. "I wonder who is spoiling Hoppity?" Daddy smiled.

"Well," said Mommy, "It's not every day we have a
thunderstorm." Then she added, "After all, this has been
Hoppity's first thunderstorm, so I think he deserves a
special treat."

Hoppity stayed awake until he had told Tufty all about the noisy thunder. "Thunder isn't really a big giant stamping about the clouds," he whispered to Tufty. "It's just a big loud bang in the sky, louder even than I can make with my drum." He wasn't sure if Tufty was really listening so he added quickly, "Anyway, it can't hurt us and it doesn't last long." Then he closed his eyes and fell fast asleep.